951039

THE BOY WHO LOVED
MORNING

by Shannon K. Jacobs   Illustrated by Michael Hays

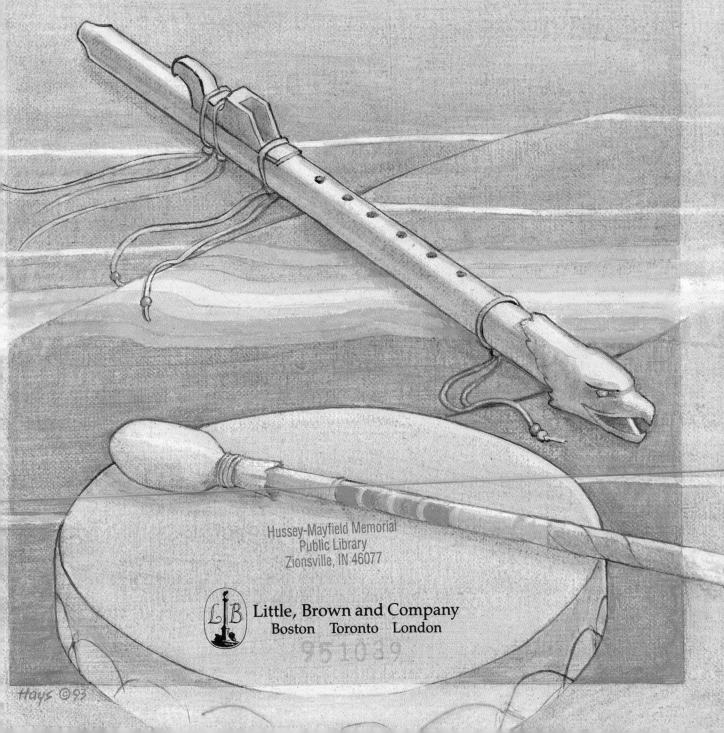

LJB Little, Brown and Company
Boston   Toronto   London

Hays ©93

AUTHOR'S NOTE

This story grew out of my great love and respect for Native American spiritual traditions, especially those teaching the connection of all life. It does not depict any specified tribe.

First Edition

Library of Congress Cataloging-in-Publication Data

Jacobs, Shannon K.
   The boy who loved morning / by Shannon K. Jacobs ;
illustrated by Michael Hays. — 1st ed.
      p.   cm.
   Summary: Only after he has learned the difference between honoring morning and changing it to suit his own pride can Boy find the perfect name for himself.
   ISBN 0-316-45556-3
   1. Indians of North America — Juvenile fiction.
[1. Indians of North America — Fiction.   2. Names, Personal — Fiction.
3. Morning — Fiction.]   I. Hays, Michael, 1956–   ill.
II. Title.
PZ7.J152537Bo   1993
[E] — dc20   91-32046

10 9 8 7 6 5 4 3 2 1

WOR

Published simultaneously in Canada
by Little, Brown & Company (Canada) Limited

Printed in the United States of America

Calligraphy by Barbara Bash

Illustrations were painted in acrylic on linen canvas that was primed with acrylic gesso. Photographic references were used for the main characters. Original art is the same size as reproduced.

To my parents, Virginia and Dale Kittel,
who led the way
with generous humor, spirit, and heart

S.K.J.

To the singing and drumming and dancing of All Nations

M.H.

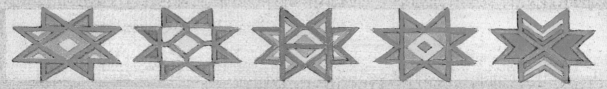

It was dark when Boy rose from his bed. Very quietly he wrapped a blanket around himself and tucked his flute inside his belt. He stood for a moment in the middle of the tipi, listening to his mother, sister, and grandfather sleep. Then he opened the flap and stepped outside.

Walking barefoot through the cool sand, Boy followed the steep rocky trail to the mesa. When he reached the top, he spread his blanket and sat facing the eastern sky.

"Thank you for this morning, Great Spirit," he prayed silently. Picking up his flute, Boy took a deep breath and blew one sweet note.

Morning answered Boy's greeting with a golden smile that lit up the sky behind the mountains. Boy's heart filled with joy.

Hearing a long sigh behind him, Boy turned. There sat his three friends — Coyote, Crow, and Snake.

"Your beautiful song woke morning," said Coyote.

Snake bobbed his head in agreement. Crow hopped closer to Boy, very interested in the flute. Boy held it out for Crow's inspection. The bird's sharp eyes saw Boy's hawk totem carved into the flute. She admired that kind of detail.

"Where did you get this?" Crow asked.

"Grandfather made it for me," Boy explained.

Snake said, "You play with enchantment." Boy smiled. He was not used to praise from Snake. Usually Snake listened but did not speak.

Coyote said, "What a fine gift for honoring morning."

"Is that what it is for?" asked Crow. She liked everything to have a use.

In reply, Boy put the warm wood to his lips, and music soared across the valley. Crow hopped to the edge of the mesa and watched the new morning respond to Boy's song, warming purple shadows in the valley.

"Ah," murmured Crow, nodding her shiny head. "That is what it is for."

As Boy played his flute, Coyote leaned against him, enjoying the power of the music, and Boy felt Coyote's warm coat on his bare skin. It was as if the music from Boy's flute threaded them all together, even cold-blooded Snake.

Moments later Boy opened his eyes and laid down the flute. His friends were gone. Morning had come. Feeling purified, complete, he slowly climbed down the trail and walked toward home.

With the music of morning still in his heart, Boy did not see Grandfather until he almost walked into him. The old man sat among the
sacred stones, praying softly, wrapped in his buffalo robe.

Boy started to change his path. But he stopped when he heard
Grandfather say, "My heart aches for my people, Great Spirit. Without
the buffalo we have no food, no clothing, no shelter. Please guide the
buffalo back to our hunting grounds."

Sadness pierced Boy's heart as he remembered stories his people

told about the great herds of buffalo they had hunted. Once there were
so many of the huge beasts that they shook the earth for days as they
thundered over the plains. Now they were disappearing quickly, as
were the antelope. And more and more white settlers were pulling
wagons onto the hunting grounds, claiming the land as theirs.

   Where he had been so proud moments ago, to have been greeted by
morning, Boy now felt that this gift was small, not worthy of mention.
He slipped quietly around Grandfather.

That evening, when Grandfather returned from another long council meeting, he asked, "Did you greet morning with your flute, Grandson?"

"Yes, Grandfather," Boy answered. He wanted to tell him everything, especially that morning had answered him. But just then Black Hawk, a scout and messenger, asked to speak with Grandfather right away. So Boy bit his tongue to remind himself not to wag it with too much talk. After all, the tribe was in danger, and Grandfather had many others to listen to.

But who besides Grandfather knew of his love for morning? He and Boy used to greet mornings together, rising before light and sitting high on the mesa. Grandfather had told Boy a long time ago, "There is no greater gift than to love. Always celebrate what you love." For the past three seasons, though, Grandfather had been too busy, so Boy had learned to celebrate alone.

Now Grandfather seemed far away as he said, "It is near the time for your naming, Grandson. Your mother and sister look forward to the ceremony. They wish to invite all our people."

Boy nodded eagerly. He also was looking forward to it. After his family presented names to the council, a final choice would be made at the ceremony in two moons. A person's naming was a very important event. Sometimes the choice of a name could affect a person's future.

Since the naming ceremony was two moons off, Boy tried to put it out of his mind and concentrate on his flute playing. But sometimes, as he played his music to honor morning, he imagined names for himself.

"Son of Dawn," Boy whispered, to hear how this name would sound. Coyote howled the name into the valley, and it came back in echoes. Coyote liked the name. Crow fluffed her feathers impatiently. She felt that names, in general, were foolish. Snake, though, seemed to give great consideration to how the name traveled in the sky. His tongue flickered in the air, tasting it, but he made no comment.

As spring dawns came earlier, Boy rose earlier to greet them. He arrived on the mesa just as pink-orange clouds broke into tongues of warm fire. Boy's three friends — Coyote, Crow, and Snake — always joined him and listened to the music. Boy would find them gone when he finished his salute to dawn, but they would be there the next day.

As each day grew longer, Boy felt more and more sure of his flute playing. He was very eager to play for his grandfather, but he decided to wait until he could play perfectly and truly honor the old man's gift.

One night Boy could not sleep at all. He rose hours before dawn and took his flute to the mesa. Feeling at peace with the night, he played a quiet, respectful greeting. But as he played, he began to imagine the bright colors of dawn. Without knowing it, he changed his music. The quiet notes that had flowed with starlight now began to leap across the sky.

Boy stood, flinging off his blanket. Up went his flute to the sky as he sang to the stars. Down went his flute to the ground as he blew music into the sleeping earth. Around and around he danced, calling morning in a frenzy of excitement.

The first bubble of dawn rose seconds later, as if puffed out of a pipe. It rode up the black sky in golden splendor, then burst into a ball of fire.

Boy's excitement grew as he saw this, and he danced and played louder and faster. When he saw more bubbles of dawn rise and burst into explosions of gold, he threw back his head and cried, "I did it! I made morning come early!"

Exhausted, Boy fell onto his blanket. As he closed his eyes to sleep, he saw the shapes of his three friends, Coyote, Crow, and Snake.

"Your song wakes morning early. How powerful you must feel," Coyote said.

"Yes," Boy agreed happily. He imagined how proud this would make Grandfather. Then he sat up and said to his friends, "Wakes Morning Early. Is that a worthy name for me?"

But his friends did not answer.

"Call it to the valley," Boy ordered Coyote. "Then we will hear it sung in many voices."

So Coyote howled the name, "Wakes Morning Early," down into the valley and the echoes returned. Boy laughed, pleased at the sound. But he did not ask his friends what they thought. And he did not notice

their silence as they sat stiffly on the edge of the mesa.

During the next moon, Boy went to the mesa every night, hours before dawn. Little by little, bubble by bubble, he coaxed dawn to appear earlier each time.

"The power of your song changes the harmony of day and night," Coyote remarked.

Boy smiled, filled with pride. As Crow stood at the mesa edge and listened to the squawks of confused birds in the valley, she said, "My feathered brothers and sisters do not understand why the sky lights up at night."

"Because I made it happen!" Boy shouted, dancing in triumph. He did not notice how his three friends moved away from him as if they were afraid.

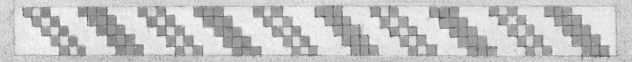

Now that he was sure of his ability, Boy was eager to play his flute for Grandfather. Then he thought of a way he could truly impress the old man. I will play at the naming ceremony, he decided, feeling full of courage. He asked Grandfather for permission.

"It will make me very happy to have my only grandson honor this important ceremony," Grandfather answered. Boy almost shouted with joy. Everyone in the tribe would be there to witness his amazing power over morning.

Finally the day of the naming ceremony arrived. The camp overflowed with people, horses, and tipis. Soon the evening feast was past and the sky was pure black. Shimmering stars pierced the thick darkness.

Boy's heart drummed fast when he thought of how dramatic his performance would be. He had decided to call for a full sunrise at midnight.

As a warm hand touched his shoulder, Boy spun around to see Grandfather smiling down at him. "Go, my grandson, and honor this ceremony with beauty and grace," he said.

Boy walked to a clearing where many groups of people sat. He lifted the flute to his lips and looked at the hushed crowd. The moment he saw Grandfather's shining eyes, Boy began to play.

Slow, sweet notes floated from Boy's flute and hovered above the crowd in long breaths. An "ahhhhh" escaped from the people as they admired the beauty of the music. Boy did not see faces anymore as he played. He felt the crowd's presence as if it were a huge, friendly beast sprawled out before him.

With his flute he sang to all sacred directions, to earth and to all her creatures, and to sun, moon, and stars.

Then Boy left the soft quiet of night and imagined the burning face of dawn. His speed increased. His feet danced faster on earth, calling for dawn. Soon the notes were shorter, sharper, like quick bird cries.

People stood up, feeling the wild rhythms. One by one they began dancing to Boy's fast music. They leapt and kicked and pounded the earth as fast as stampeding buffalo.

Seeing this effect on his people, Boy felt a thrill of excitement, and he imagined another name for himself. The name was Midnight Fire.

No one else saw the first bubble of golden light float up the black sky.

Only Boy, who was watching for it, noticed it. He played more wildly. More bubbles appeared and burst into small puffs of golden fire.

Then Boy's heart jumped when he saw the eastern sky light up. Flames of golden yellow danced across the sky as if grass fires had been set among the clouds.

"Look!" someone shouted. The people stopped dancing. They stared with open mouths at the most amazing sight they had ever seen — the sun rising at midnight.

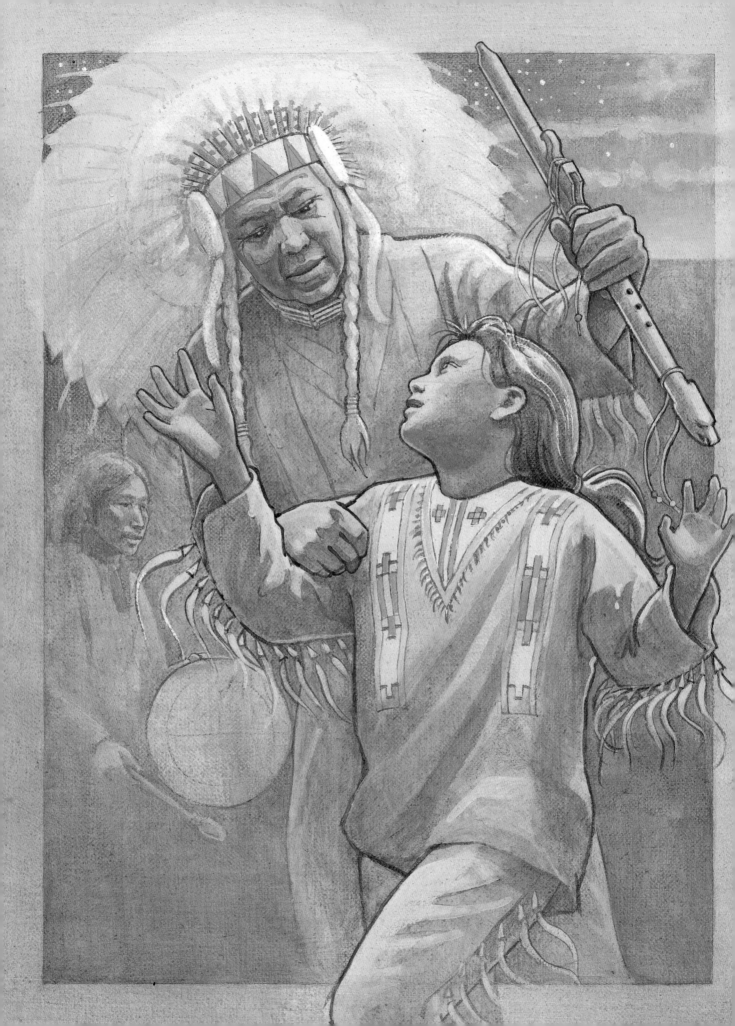

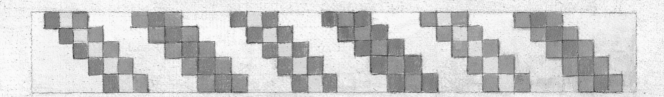

Boy was lost in the sound of his flute and the sight of fire in the sky. When Grandfather appeared before him, speaking, Boy did not hear.

Suddenly Grandfather grabbed the flute out of Boy's hands. As silence fell, the sun sank behind the mountains, taking all the midnight light with it.

Boy, dizzy with his power, tried to keep dancing. But Grandfather clutched his arm and held it tightly. Boy swayed against the old man as if he were weak from fasting.

"Did you see it, Grandfather?" Boy cried. "Did you see what I did?"

Grandfather did not answer. He led Boy through the bewildered people and headed for the council lodge. Boy looked up at the old man, eager to hear his words of praise, to see his proud smile. But as the fires lit up Grandfather's face, Boy saw only shame and disappointment.

It felt to Boy as if his heart had been crushed. He wanted to crash to his knees and cry, or to run, anything not to see Grandfather's face. With a fast movement, Boy broke free from Grandfather's grasp and ran through the crowd, darting in and out among the people like a rabbit dodging rocks.

Soon he was running up the mesa. He shot up the path and, gasping for air, fell on his face when he reached the top.

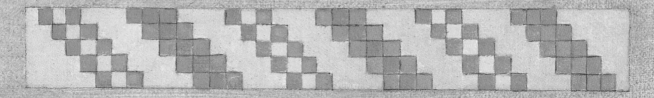

Boy opened his eyes. His three friends — Coyote, Crow, and Snake — sat beside him. As the memory of Grandfather's face came back to him, Boy covered his own face.

"Did your people enjoy the sun rising at midnight?" Coyote asked.

Boy moaned and shrugged his shoulders helplessly.

"And Grandfather," Coyote continued, "what did he say?"

Boy shook his head. "He did not speak. But his face. Oh, how I shamed him." He pounded the earth in frustration. "But what did I do?"

With a loud sigh, Boy got to his feet and walked to the edge of the mesa. He could see the small fires lit for the naming ceremony in the valley.

Crow hopped next to Boy so she too looked over the valley. "Why

do your people hold so many ceremonies?" she asked in her usual
sharp way.

Boy felt irritated with Crow's question, but he responded, "We give
thanks to Great Spirit. And we honor the sacred earth and kinship of
all creatures."

"Surely then your flute sang thanks to Great Spirit for abundant
berries and roots and good buffalo hunts?" Crow asked as she hopped
in front of him.

Boy started to speak, but he could not.

Snake lifted his head. "And of course you honored the harmony of
earth with the song of your flute?"

Boy shook his head slowly.

Coyote spoke from behind him. "What did the sweet music of your flute celebrate, my friend?"

Boy was quiet for a long time. His patient friends waited, not moving. Finally he turned to them and said, "I did not give thanks to Great Spirit. And I did not honor the sacred earth and kinship of all creatures." Boy's three friends moved closer to him. Their loyalty gave him strength and understanding.

"That is Grandfather's shame," Boy whispered. "I honored only my power."

Coyote said gently, "He must hear, from your own lips, what you have learned."

"Yes, I must return," Boy agreed. He turned to his companions. "Thank you, my friends."

After he prayed for a long time, Boy climbed down the trail and walked back to his village. The fires had burned down, and the people were sleeping. Without a sound, Boy entered his tipi, lay down on his bed, and fell asleep.

It seemed to Boy that he had just closed his eyes when he felt a hand shake him. He sat up quickly. It was still dark. Grandfather squatted near him.

"Come, Grandson," he whispered, "let us greet morning."

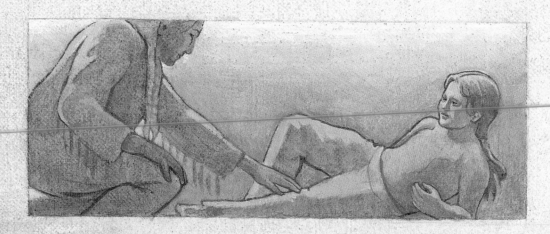

Together they walked up the steep trail to the mesa top. At the edge of the mesa they sat down, facing east. Just as a soft, golden light appeared along the horizon, Boy felt Grandfather place something in his hands. It was the flute. "Play," said Grandfather.

Boy put the flute to his lips and played a quiet song full of joy for the beauty of morning. When dawn slowly lit up the sky behind the mountains, Boy set down his flute. He felt the new morning fill him with hope.

"That was beautiful," Grandfather said. He gestured to the sky, then to the valley below. "That, too, is beautiful. What if someone changed this beautiful creation to suit his own pride?"

Boy felt shame burn his cheeks, but he answered softly, "He would upset the sacred harmony of earth."

"And would it be perfect, for all living things, as it is now?" Grandfather asked.

"No," Boy answered, shaking his head, "it would not." Then he vowed, "I will not wake the sun early ever again, Grandfather. I will sing only praises to the morning."

Grandfather nodded, looking very tired, Boy thought. Then something unexpected happened. A tiny smile pulled Grandfather's lips up at the corners. As hard as he tried, Grandfather could not stop himself from smiling. Then he was laughing loudly, covering his mouth and rocking back and forth.

"You always do things in big, big ways, Grandson," he said. "Who else would tease the sun out at midnight to impress their old grandfather?" And he pulled Boy into his arms and hugged him tightly.

When he released Boy and wiped his eyes, Grandfather said, "I have not been a good teacher for you lately, my grandson, and I regret that. Our people have many difficult times ahead. Our way of life is in great danger."

Grandfather stared over the valley, his brow wrinkled in worry. Boy sat with him quietly, respectful of the old man's thoughts.

Then Boy asked, "Will I receive a name, Grandfather?"

"What have you wished for?" Grandfather asked.

Boy thought about the names he had wanted — Son of Dawn, Wakes

Morning Early, and Midnight Fire. Each one would tell a different story. But which one should he choose?

He turned to his three friends, who had appeared at the edge of the mesa. They remained silent, watching him. Boy searched Grandfather's patient eyes for an answer, but there was none. Then, as a cool wind whistled across the mesa, a new name came to Boy. The right name.

"Morning Song," Boy said. "That is the name I wish for."

The old man was quiet for what seemed like a very long time. Boy lowered his head, afraid he did not deserve such a name. When he finally looked up, he saw Grandfather smiling.

"Welcome, Morning Song," said his grandfather.

Boy's name became Morning Song that moment, and as his wise old grandfather blessed the name, the sun rose above the mountains, warming the mesa top.

Coyote howled the name into the valley, and it returned in many voices singing like flutes. Snake tested the sound with his tongue and nodded, satisfied. And even Crow had to agree that it was a very good name for a boy who loved morning.

3